~~Mama's Day at Work~~
Bunny Business

Lori Richmond

SCHOLASTIC PRESS • NEW YORK

Library of Congress Cataloging-in-Publication Data available
ISBN 978-0-545-92590-7 • 10 9 8 7 6 5 4 3 2 1   20 21 22 23 24 • Printed in Malaysia   108 • First edition, January 2020
The art was created in ink and watercolor, and composited digitally. No bunnies were harmed in the making of this book.
The text was set in 20 pt. Kepler Std Medium and Kepler Std Medium Italic. The display type was set in Kepler Std Caption.
Art direction by Marijka Kostiw. Book design by Lori Richmond and Marijka Kostiw.

FOR HOLDEN AND COOPER,

SNACK-SEEKING, DRY-ERASE DRAWING,
AND ARCADE GAMING DUO OF 195 BROADWAY

AND FOR CARLEY AND DAVID,
WHO ALWAYS WELCOMED THEM IN THE OFFICE

It's Monday morning when Mama finds out the bunnysitter is sick.

Papa just left . . .

school is closed . . .

and the neighbors
are in Bunbados.

"I can't leave you alone
while I'm at work," said Mama.
"What am I going to do?"

"I'll go with you!" said Bunny.

"Hop along," said Mama.

"Or we'll be late."

And they zoom off to the big city.

"Let's go look at the art!" said Bunny.

"Not now," said Mama.

"I'm hungry," said Bunny.

"I'm late for a meeting," said Mama. "We'll get a snack when I'm done."

"But I'm hungry *now*," said Bunny.

"Stay here in my office and draw," said Mama.

"I'll be close by where I can keep an ear on you."

So THIS is what Mama does at work all day!

After a while, Mama still hasn't come back.

Bunny waits.

And waits.

My tummy is so rumbly.

And waits.

She's been gone forever!

I'll go look for Mama.

Instead, Bunny finds . . .

SNACKS
$1.00
Carrot Crunchies
Carro-Stix
Carrot Stix
Caritos
Fluffy Puffs
Bun Chips
Salsa
HOP.Os
Bunyuns
Original
Ranch

But how can I reach the buttons? thought Bunny.

Then Bunny has a better idea . . .

. . . but I don't have any money. Now I'll never get a snack.

Then Bunny has an *even better* idea . . .

and is back in business.

"Snacks for everyone!" said Bunny.

Caritos
RANCH

Fluffy
Puffs

HOP·Os

Bunyuns

Carrot
CRUNCHIES

Bun
Chips
SALSA

CARROT
STIX

CARROTZ

HOP·Os

Bunyuns

Caritos
ORIGINAL

Fluffy
Puffs